Hamlet Goes To School

Carolyn Ashcraft

Wordseed Publishing
Hermiston, Oregon

Hamlet Goes To School

Published by:
Wordseed Publishing
650 NE 2nd Street
Hermiston, Or 97838
hashcraftz1@charter.net

ISBN 0-9755232-0-1
Library in Congress Control Number: 2004093609

This book is dedicated to my granddaughter Alexis, who gave me encouragement and advice, and my daughter Dianna who believed in me.

Love,

Grandma-Mom

1
The Piper's Curse!

Kirby Piper hated broccoli, worms, and books! His mom could fix him oodles of other green stuff to eat. His dad could bait Kirby's hook on fishing trips, but books? Well, he was just plain stuck with books!

In fact, books haunted him from everywhere. In the living room, they clung to the shelves of tall oak bookcases on each side of the television. Kirby called them book caves. Books of various sizes and shapes lurked down at him when he watched his TV shows, as if waiting to silently pounce on him!

His mom thought she was being sneaky by putting books on the round glass coffee table. She figured Kirby would have to move them whenever he used the surface for his race cars and maybe read a few of them. Well, she was right about Kirby moving them, but wrong about him reading them. He would just shove them over to give him room to play.

In his bedroom, books were his worst enemy. They were scattered everywhere. His dad had made shelves for books, but Kirby had used those for his toys. He wanted to lie in bed and look over at what he called his good stuff. The last thing he wanted to see before he went to sleep was a book!

The majority of his bothersome books were under his bed. He used his blue and red plaid bedspread to hide them from sight. The bad thing was, however, when he lost something. He'd have to reach under there and risk dragging one of the dreaded things out. They all seemed to be screaming, "Read me! Read me!"

If this wasn't bad enough, it seems the family had the Piper Curse. His Mom told him about it last year. According to her, this so called curse had been passed down through the family for years.

"It was the Piper's family responsibility to pass on the skill and the love of reading to the next generation. All those who failed would be asking for disaster." She was not sure what

6

was meant by this so called disaster.

When Kirby questioned her, she just said for him not to worry, "no Piper had ever failed at reading." Most of the time, he thought it was a big fat fib that his parents had made up to get him to read more, but some of the time he wasn't so sure, especially when he was lying in bed at night in the dark. He could almost hear the books under the bed breathing.

Everyone in the family seemed to take the curse seriously. Each birthday or special occasion, Kirby received books from some member of his family. They all had words in them. And to Kirby that was the problem. If they had just left the words out, he might not mind reading one.

Kirby knew this year was going to be worse! He was going to start fourth grade in two days. Which meant the books in school would be fatter and the words longer. He had a feeling that he was going to learn first hand what disaster fell to those who failed to fulfill the Piper Curse.

2
Freedom Saturday

Kirby was lying on the couch upside down. His feet were draped up over the back. His brown curly hair cushioned his head pressed against the floor. Watching a cartoon, he laughed at SpongeBob getting the best of Squidward. Kirby grimaced when he heard his mother's voice.

"Kirby, you need to straighten up your room before we go to the store for school shoes," Mrs. Piper hollered from the kitchen.

She trudged into the living room with a basket of clothes under one arm and a stack of newspapers in the other.

"Mom, this is my last Saturday of freedom. Can't we go later when SpongeBob is over?" Kirby pleaded.

"No, we have too many things to do, and besides you saw that very same episode last week," Mrs. Piper reminded.

"I know, that is why I am watching it upside down. It looks completely different this way," Kirby replied with a mischievous grin.

"Well, I could have you stand on your head the next time I fix broccoli and see if it tastes completely different." Mom chuckled.

"Okay," Kirby reluctantly replied as he trudged upstairs to his room. He had his own room. Kirby's younger sister Alexis' bedroom was next door. She was five and as far as Kirby was concerned a big pest. She loved books! She even slept with her book *Sleeping Beauty*. Her parents had to read the same book to her every night or she refused to go to sleep. They had tried to get him to read to Alexis but Kirby had raised such a fuss that they had given up.

3

If you're Smart you'll get out Of Here!

Kirby looked in his mirror. *Well I guess this is what I'm going to look like as a fourth grader.*

He eyed the heavy horizontal black lines his dad had drawn on the wall with a thick magic marker. His dad had kept a record of Kirby's height on it since he was three. There was a decal of a football helmet at the five foot mark. His dad had promised to take him to a Seattle Seahawks game when his head reached that point. Kirby still had to look up at the mark but he only had a couple of inches to go before he would be hitting his dad up for that promised game.

Kirby kicked the stuff that was starting to crawl out from under his bed. He then pulled the bed covers down to the floor, punched the pillow in the stomach, and said with relief, "there that's done."

The bedroom door opened and his sister Alexis twirled into the room. She had curly hair like Kirby's, which was tied in two pony tails on each side of her head. She was wearing an old lace curtain tied around her waist, giving her the appearance, she hoped, of a ballerina.

She stopped and folded her arms in front of her and tapped her foot. "Mommy is going to buy me some new shoes too. My shoes are going to be kiddiegarter shoes."

"That's kindergarten not kiddiegarter, you dumb dumb!" snapped Kirby who was becoming more irritated by the minute.

"Who cares!" returned Alexis. "I'm going to get to go to school every day just like you. I'm going to get just as smart as you, probably smarter!"

"If you're smart, you'll get out of here and leave me alone!"

Alexis danced out of the bedroom. Her encounter with Kirby did little to dampen her cheerful spirit. Kirby could hear her continue to sing as she bounced down the hall.

4

If You Go Too Fast, Boom!

Within an hour, Kirby, Alexis and Mrs. Piper were in the shoe department at Wal-Mart. Alexis found her shoes right away. She was hopping around and hugging them.

"I'm going to show my school shoes to my new teacher. I'm going to walk into my school room the very first day real, real loud so that everybody looks at my beautiful shoes!" squealed Alexis.

Kirby rolled his eyes up at the ceiling. He didn't mind getting shoes, but he hated shoe shopping. Kirby's mom made him try on practically every shoe that was anywhere near his size. Then, she made him walk around in every one of them. Most of them had rubber strings attached to each shoe, so you had to sort of scoot along like a cross country skier. Kirby called them shoe cuffs. If you went too fast, bam, you went flying head first. And no matter what, you just don't look cool in shoe cuffs.

Kirby was on his knees putting the shoes in the box that had made the final cut as "the school shoes" when he looked up to see Lila Smithers. Kirby had spent his entire school career trying to avoid her. She had been in all his classes since Kindergarten.

She had long blond hair that she was proud to say had never been cut. Her hair went all the way down her back.

She considered herself as queen of the classroom. If she missed one word on a spelling test, she went into a tizzy. Her handwriting was perfect, no eraser holes like Kirby's and she had been reading chapter books since first grade.

"Good morning Mrs. Piper, and you too, Kirby. I see Kirby has found some shoes for school." The shrill irritating voice was Mrs. Smithers'.

Lila was a carbon copy of her mother except Mrs. Smithers' blond hair was piled up high on her head.

Lila interrupted, "We don't usually shop for shoes here. We usually go to Luxor's Boutique Shop. It's closed today. They had some sort of water pipe problem."

"Yes, poor Lila, I hope we find some shoes that will do, just until Luxor's opens again. Lila has such delicate feet," chattered Mrs. Smithers.

"It must be difficult," Mrs. Piper agreed. Kirby knew his mother found Mrs. Smithers as irritating as he did, but she was too nice to act like it. He had heard his mom and dad talking about her. She had called Mrs. Smithers pompous. When Kirby had asked what pompous meant she had scolded him for eaves dropping and told him to go play. He never did find out what pompous meant, but he figured it wasn't a compliment.

Kirby shoved his new shoes into the box as quickly as he could and headed for the checkout, followed by Alexis and his mom. If they hurried, he could still get back in time for some of his favorite shows on TV.

Kirby knew his hopes of seeing his cartoons went out the window when his mom announced, "Sorry guys, but we need to make one more special stop."

5

Finally The Box Was Open!

"Okay Mom, but is this special thing going to take long?" Kirby whined.

Kirby's mom just ignored him and kept driving. After a few blocks, she pulled into the parking lot of the post office and stopped the car.

Mom turned and looked toward the back seat and ordered, "Okay, everybody out. We have to pick up a special package."

Once inside, Mom asked the clerk for a package addressed to Kirby and Alexis Piper.

As she reached for a brown paper covered box, she sneezed. Mrs. Piper looked at the return label. "It's from your Uncle Louie."

Kirby's Uncle Louie was his dad's brother. He had moved to Alaska way before Kirby was born. Kirby had never met him in person, but had heard a lot about him. He lived miles from everywhere in Alaska in a log cabin he had built himself. He panned for gold along the river banks. His dad had called him eccentric.

His cabin walls were lined with books. He said his books insulated the walls and kept his body and heart warm.

Kirby could have bet his allowance money what was inside the box. Uncle Louie never failed to send him a package at the beginning of the school year. It was always a book. Kirby figured it was his uncle's contribution to saving him from the Piper Curse.

"Hey Mommy, how come the box has holes in it?" Alexis squealed with excitement.

On the box was written, KEEP THIS SIDE UP...LIVE...LIVE.

"Mom, look what it says!" shrieked Kirby.

The last few blocks to Kirby's house seemed to take forever. Mrs. Piper had insisted that the kids not touch the box until they arrived home. Kirby was positive she was driving slower than normal just to drive him crazy. At the sound of the engine being shut off, the kids snapped their seat belts open and within seconds they were out of the car and running to the house.

They had to wait until their mother caught up with them. Mrs. Piper sneezed several more times as she opened the front door to the house.

"I sure hope I'm not getting a cold. I don't have time for that this time of year," she sniffed.

Once inside, everyone hurried to the kitchen table where all the important business matters took place. They scrambled to move all the accumulation of the morning's activities from the table. Dishes, newspapers, a few envelopes and two Barbie dolls were quickly thrown onto the kitchen cabinet. Mrs. Piper set the package softly on the middle of the table and then handed Kirby a sharp pair of scissors.

"Here Kirby, now be real careful! You can do the honors of opening it," she said ceremoniously.

As Kirby cut the heavy strapping tape, his sister poked her head in closer and closer for a better look.

"Mom," Kirby complained, "make Alexis get her head out of the way!"

"Yes, love, get your head back. There might be something in that box that bites," she said in a teasing voice.

Finally the package was open. It contained two smaller wrapped boxes. The first was addressed to Alexis.

"It's mine, it's mine!" squealed Alexis. She quickly tore it open to find a talking book called Sleeping Beauty. "My favorite, my favorite," she squeaked as she hugged the book to her chest.

The last box to be opened had Kirby's name on it. On top of it was taped a short note. Kirby read it out loud.

Kirby this is to help you with your reading. His name is Hamlet. Love, Uncle Louie

"Hamlet must be something alive," Kirby exclaimed.

"Maybe it's a bear from Alaska," Alexis cried. "Or maybe a snake!"

Mrs. Piper shivered, "Alexis why don't we just wait and see."

Kirby could wait no longer. He opened the box as quickly as he could. He wanted to tear it open like Alexis did, but the thought of something being alive forced him to proceed slowly. As soon as he folded the flaps back, he peered down into the darkness of the box. Something looked back at him!

"I think it's a mouse!" Kirby stammered in what he hoped was a calm voice.

His mom automatically shrank back from the table a couple of feet.

Slowly all three of them crept up and

peeked into the box.

Kirby scooped up a small creature in the palms of his hands. It reminded him of a tiny furry beanie baby. Its little round black eyes seem to stare right at him. "I think it's a hamster! He slowly and carefully folded his fingers back so that everyone could see it from all sides. After close inspection, everyone agreed it was indeed a hamster.

"Why do you suppose Uncle Louie named it Hamlet?" questioned Kirby.

"I remember Uncle Louie was always reading plays by a man named William Shakespeare. One of the characters Mr. Shakespeare wrote about was a guy named Hamlet," reported Mrs. Piper.

"Was Hamlet a hamster?" Kirby questioned.

"No," she laughed, "he was a person and he led a real adventurous life."

Mrs. Piper walked over to the kitchen cabinet and reached for an empty glass.

"The first thing I'm going to do is to take some vitamin C," she said, half talking to herself as she fumbled in a drawer for a small bottle of vitamins. "I can't be getting a cold now, not with one more mouth to feed in the house and just where is this little fellow going to sleep?"

"He can sleep in my bed with me!" Kirby quickly responded.

"Not on my freshly laundered sheets!" Mom exclaimed. "I think one of those big plastic tubs in the garage should fit the bill. Kirby, you can put it by your bed. As for food, I think we can find something in the vegetable bin in the fridge."

"Maybe they eat cookies," broke in Alexis. "Maybe we should start baking cookies, chocolate chip cookies!"

Kirby's mom found a tall square plastic tub for Hamlet. They shredded the newspaper on the kitchen counter and used it to line the bottom of the tub. Kirby searched the fridge.

After Hamlet was safely bedded down, the household returned to their normal routine. Mom started supper and Alexis went off to play with her new book.

Kirby set the tub beside his bed in his room and then flopped onto his own bed and stared down at Hamlet. His fur was a warm brown color. Kirby thought, he was just the shade of his dad's morning coffee after he put a little cream in it.

As terrific as Hamlet appeared to be, Kirby wondered how Uncle Louie could ever think a hamster could help with his reading.

6

With Each Noise Kirby Cringed

"Kirby, you are not going to be late for school your very first day! If I have to come up there one more time and you are not out of that bed I am calling your father!" Mrs. Piper's voice vibrated into Kirby's ears from the kitchen downstairs.

Now she was standing on the stairs with her arms folded across her chest. "I told you last night to go to sleep earlier. Kirby, tonight we'll subtract one half hour from your bedtime!" scolded Mrs. Piper.

Kirby rolled out of bed, smacking his head into the tub where Hamlet was sleeping peacefully. The tub rolled over bumping into the bat propped against the night stand making a loud thud as it hit the wall.

Alexis came dancing through the doorway. "Kirby, look at my school clothes, Mommy says I look like a school princess. Mommy didn't even have to wake me up. Your room is sure messy. My room is as straight as a string. Hey, Kirby where's Hamlet?" rattled on Alexis without taking a breath.

Irritated, Kirby jumped up quickly. His feet got tangled in the covers and he was flung back into his bed. His head was sticking out over the side, practically in Hamlet's tub.

Alexis laughed and clapped her hands. "You're funny Kirby!" she squealed.

Kirby was horrified when he could not see Hamlet. He franticly dug through the shredded newspaper in the tub. Hamlet was gone!

"Don't move Alexis," he whispered. "You might step on Hamlet!"

"Why are we whispering?" said Alexis, not lowering her voice.

"We don't want to scare him and you are not whispering." Kirby moaned a little louder.

With a sinking feeling, Kirby looked at his bed with its jumbled sheets and blankets.

"Alexis, I think he must be under the bed!

You're going to have to crawl under there and look for Hamlet. You have to be real careful not to touch any of my stuff under there, especially the books. If one of those books falls on him he'll be a goner," Kirby explained.

"Okay," said Alexis feeling very important.

She dove under the bed. The only thing Kirby could see was the soles of her new shoes. "Here Hammy Hammy, here Hammy," called Alexis. She thought this was a great game.

"It's dark under here. I need a flashlight." She giggled from under the bed.

Kirby rummaged in his over-flowing toy box until he pulled out a Batman flashlight. As he switched it on, it cast a faint black bat surrounded by a yellow circle on the wall.

"This will have to do," he said as he shoved the flashlight under the bed.

"Hey, cool!" rang out Alexis' voice. "Looks like I'm in a spooky dark cave with a real big bat. I'm Bat Lady!"

"Never mind that, hurry and find Hamlet," groaned Kirby.

Kirby could hear things banging into each other under the bed. With each noise, he cringed. He had visions of Hamlet being smashed like a pancake with one of the heavy storybooks.

In a few more long agonizing minutes,

Alexis backed out from under the bed. Clutched in both her hands was Hamlet. With a look of pure pride, she handed him to Kirby.

"I had to crawl on my elbows to get out!" said Alexis proudly. "I'm pretty sure Hamlet was reading one the books."

Kirby carefully grasped Hamlet and placed him back safely into the plastic tub.

"Okay, now get out of here, get out! I've got to get ready for school!" Kirby yelled to his sister.

"Okay, but you're 'posed to be grateful to me for saving Hamlet," Alexis protested as she stomped from the room.

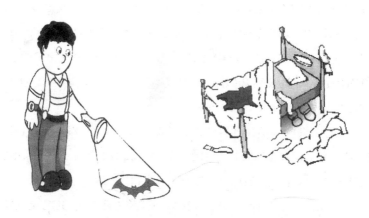

7

You're the Bravest Person in the Whole World!

Kirby's mom took Alexis to school by car. Kirby had insisted on walking the one block to school on his own. He wanted to walk with his next door neighbor and best friend, Frankie Sanchez. They had been buddies since the beginning of second grade when Frankie's family had moved from California.

When Kirby and Frankie arrived at school, they saw almost as many parents as students. For some reason, which made no sense to Kirby, parents seem to worry if their kids made it to school the first day. If kids were going to skip school, it sure wouldn't be the first day, he thought. This was the day to size everybody up, especially your teacher.

Kirby and Frankie headed for room 18. Their teacher was to be Mrs. Hensley. At least Frankie was going to be in his class.

Along the way, they passed a couple of kids headed in the direction of the kindergarten.

They were crying. Holding their hands were their parent's who were sniffling and dabbing their own eyes.

I don't get it, thought Kirby. It should be the big kids crying on the first day of school. In kindergarten, they get a cookie break and parents get all day to lie around while their kids are in school.

After passing several classrooms, Kirby and Frankie reached room 18. Kirby called it his cell for the rest of the year. He reluctantly opened the door and there she was, the queen of the classroom.

Lila Smithers was taking off her pink flowered backpack. Oh no, thought Kirby, she is in my class again! She was a royal pain!

"Hi Kirby," she gushed.

"Hi Kirby," Frankie said in a voice that imitated Lila's.

"Knock it off, Frankie, or you're going to get your first bloody nose of the school year!" Kirby said angrily.

Trying to ignore Lila, Kirby took his seat. Mrs. Hensley had already assigned seats and had placed name tags on the student's desks.

The bell rang and Kirby knew his summer was officially over.

Mrs. Hensley seemed pretty cool, at least

for a teacher. She was wearing a blue denim jumper and around her neck hung a big wooden necklace. A carved elephant dangled from it. Mrs. Hensley had described her picture-taking safari in Africa and had stood within feet of real wild lions.

The last bell finally rang. It couldn't have been too soon for Kirby. He felt totally wasted. He wasn't used to getting up so early in the morning. He had almost fallen asleep twice that afternoon. He had been watching the clock for at least ten minutes as the clock slowly ticked its way to 3:30.

Mrs. Hensley insisted on standing at the door to tell each student goodbye. Kirby figured it was to keep them all from trampling each other as they ran out the door. She told them they could either give her a hug or handshake goodbye.

Kirby chose to give her a handshake. Lila, of course, gave her a hug and then she told her she was the very best teacher she had ever had in her life. During the hug, Lila got her hair all tangled in Mrs. Hensley's necklace.

Kirby hurried through the building to pick up Alexis at her classroom and walk her home. Kirby had promised his mom he would not forget to pick her up.

Just as he was approaching her classroom, he saw Alexis crying outside her door. She had one shoe on and one shoe off. Two boys, who looked like second graders, were playing catch with it. Kirby ran up inbetween them.

"Hey guys, unless you want to wear that shoe in your mouth, you better take off!" Kirby said in his toughest voice.

The boys quickly dropped the shoe and took off running. He could see them run smack into the playground monitor, Mrs. Steel.

He turned his attention to Alexis. He bent down to put her shoe on her foot. "How did they get your shoe in the first place?" Kirby said gently.

"Oh Kirby," sniffed Alexis. "You're the bravest person in the whole world! You're braver than Superman and Sticker-man and Batman. I was just dancing and my foot went up in the air and my shoe went up in the air too, only higher. My foot came down but my shoe stayed up. Then those big boys grabbed it."

"It's okay. I'm glad I'm braver than Stickerman. Come on, let's go home."

He held her hand as they walked toward home. Alexis' shoes stomped loudly down the sidewalk.

8
Hamlet Must Go!

By the time they had reached the house Alexis had completely forgotten her adventure with the shoe.

"Mommy, Mommy," she yelled. "I have the bestest teacher in the whole world. Her name is Miss Cook, but she doesn't cook 'cause she is a teacher. She eats in a room called the staff room. She said I could call her teacher if I forget her name, but I'm not gonna ever forget her name. Miss Cook, Miss Cook, Miss Cook, see I won't ever forget it. I said it a whole bunch of times today so I wouldn't forget it. Just before we went home, Miss Cook said I had practiced her name enough. She said I was a real fast learner." Alexis finally stopped and took a breath.

"I'm Ahchoo…Ahchoo….proud of you Lamb Chop," said Mrs. Piper. "How was your day, Kirby?"

"Well, just take a guess who is in my class? Just take a guess! You'll never guess, never in a million years. You'd say Kirby, not in a million would you have another class with Lila Smithers. Well, you'd be wrong. Guess who sits right in front of me? You guessed it, Lila Smithers."

"Now Kirby, you are both in fourth grade. She will probably be completely different this year. Girls grow up real fast in fourth grade. You and she will probably be the best of friends in no time," said Mrs. Piper, trying to sound convincing.

Kirby made gagging sounds as he headed for the refrigerator. "I'm starving to death; you know I haven't had anything to eat since lunch. That school lunch was yucky and they hardly give us any time to eat then this lady is always running around saying, hurry up, hurry up and eat. Then you have to raise your hand when you are done and want to leave. My stomach is saying feed me, feed me!" Kirby grumbled as he opened the refrigerator.

"Why do they want you to hurry and eat?"

inquired Mrs. Piper.

"Cause Mr. Fender has to have time to mop up all the smushed food on the floor before Ms. Fudge needs the cafeteria for a gym. Some of the kids are real slobs," Kirby said with an air of authority on school matters. "Mr. Fender's real nice. He pretends to steal the dessert from our trays."

Mrs. Piper headed to the bathroom with a stack of clean towels.

Alexis started singing a confusing version of the alphabet song.

"Mom," yelled Kirby, "make Alexis shut up and quit singing. She is giving me a headache!"

Mom called from another room, "Kirby, you need to show a little more understanding with your sister."

Kirby gave his sister a dirty look as he grabbed some grapes. Then he stomped upstairs singing, "I hate school, I hate school. High ho the derry-o, I hate school!"

Kirby was sitting on his bed feeling sorry for himself and munching on the grapes when Alexis hopped into his bedroom.

"Didn't they teach you to knock in kindergarten?" Kirby bellowed. "I'm in fourth grade now and I need my privacy. I'm going to put a big sign on that door that says, No Sister Allowed!"

Alexis ignored Kirby's remarks. "Hey Kirby, we studied the letter A today. A is for Alice. She is an anteater that lives far away. We have to bring something to school tomorrow that starts with the letter A. What's something that starts with A?"

"Alabama," Kirby spat back.

"Mommy, Mommy," Alexis yelled as she headed down to the living room. "Do we have any Alabamas I can take to school tomorrow?"

That evening at supper, Kirby's mom had fixed his favorite meal—macaroni and cheese with pigs in a blanket—and Alexis' special dessert, chocolate pudding.

"Guess what, Mommy? Guess what I'm going to take to school tomorrow that starts with an A? Just guess!" demanded Alexis.

"I have no idea, Lamb Chop. Let me think. Hum, I just can't think of a thing that starts with an A," Mom said with a smile.

"Well, I'm taking me. Get it, me, Alexis. I start with an A, so I'm taking me." Alexis laughed as if she had made the funniest joke in the world.

Mom and Dad laughed. "I think that is very clever of you," they both agreed.

Kirby's last pig was sliding down his throat to "his happy hunting ground" as Dad called it, when his Mom looked at Kirby and said, "Kirby I have something unpleasant to tell you." She took a deep breath and continued. "I went to the doctor today. He said I do not have a cold. He said I am allergic to things with fur."

"But Mom," burst out Kirby, "you don't even have a fur coat!"

Then as if a Kirby had sat on a tack, he jumped up and cried, "Hamlet?"

"Yes, it's Hamlet. I can't even go upstairs without sneezing. I'm sorry," sniffed Mrs. Piper, "but Hamlet must go!"

9

What has gotten into Hamlet?

That night after supper, it was reluctantly decided to ask Mrs. Hensley to talk to her students. His mom had suggested that maybe one of them could adopt Hamlet. Kirby sat and listened while his mother talked to Mrs. Hensley on the phone. He sat whimpering on the stairs and Alexis was out right howling.

"Yes, I see," said Mrs. Piper. "I understand. Thank you. Goodbye."

Mrs. Piper put the phone down. "Well Kirby, it looks like you can keep Hamlet. You just have to keep him at school. Mrs. Hensley said you can keep his cage on the shelf in the back of the classroom and you can be in charge of his care." She paused for a second and then continued. "I'd say it's time to buy Hamlet a real cage."

Kirby jumped up and down with excitement and gave his mom a high five. "I'm going to go up and tell Hamlet right now he's going to school!" Kirby raced up the stairs taking two of them at a time.

The following day Kirby's mom drove him to school. The cage was far too big for him to carry that distance. Kirby figured to make up for evicting Hamlet, Mom bought the best cage in the pet store. It was called a hamster sanctuary.

Mrs. Hensley said he could be the zookeeper of the hamsters, even though they had only one hamster. His desk was right in front of the cage. Mrs. Hensley told Kirby as long as he got his work done and Hamlet didn't distract the class, they could both stay there.

After lunch, it was D.E.A.R. This was not Kirby's favorite time of the day. It stood for "drop everything and read." Mrs. Hensley insisted everyone get a book and read for a solid twenty minutes. Well, he had to pretend to be reading for the entire twenty minutes. He would read some, skip some, and look at pictures.

Mrs. Hensley said that Kirby could hold Hamlet while he read. So, he placed Hamlet on his shoulder and got out a book. Stumbling through a couple of sentences, he gave up and turned the page before he finished reading it.

"Ow!" Kirby screamed. Hamlet bit him on the neck. It hadn't really hurt much, but it had startled him.

"Kirby, is there a problem over there?" inquired Mrs. Hensley.

"No, no problem. I just pinched my finger in the lid of my desk," Kirby fibbed.

Kirby didn't want to lose the privilege of having Hamlet out of his cage. *What in the world has gotten into Hamlet! he* wondered.

Kirby lost his place in the book, so he returned back to the first page. After reading the first few sentences, his fingers moved to turn the page when Hamlet once more inched toward Kirby's bare neck. Kirby jerked his fingers back and continued reading.

Kirby began to think Hamlet knew when he was fake reading. Once more when Kirby turned the page too fast, Hamlet nibbled on his neck. Kirby didn't yell this time, but the nibble didn't feel very good!

As Kirby put Hamlet back in his cage, he could have sworn Hamlet winked at him. He knelt down close to the cage and looked eye to eye with Hamlet. He saw two little black eyes that soon closed as he curled into a ball and fell asleep.

10

Something Made his Blood Turn Cold!

It was Tuesday, PE day. Kirby did not look forward to Tuesday. The gym teacher was Ms. Fudge. She had put in 20 years in the Marines and had started on a second career as a PE teacher. She was built like a shoe box with feet. Her arms had so many muscles, they refused to lay flat by her sides. It gave her the appearance that she was getting ready to take off and fly. She gave orders like she had been used to in the Marine Corps. Ms. Fudge soon found out, however, that students don't obey orders as well as the Marines do.

Her favorite PE activity was the obstacle course, which she set up in the gym. The kids called it the "obstacle curse." The students had to do summersaults, jump rope, run laps, push ups, set ups and the feared rope which hung from a big steel beam running across the ceiling of the gym. Attached to the very top of the rope was a red dusty ribbon. In the entire history of the school, no one had touched the ribbon.

Ms. Fudge would stand below as each student in turn climbed as high as their muscles or guts would let them. She would then count each hand pull. The record of the school was 15, which put the climber about half way up the rope. That was done by Johnny Horton, who years later tried out for the Seattle Seahawks football team.

Kirby was holding Hamlet when Mrs. Hensley asked the class to clear their desks for PE. He quickly stashed Hamlet in his cage, so much in a hurry that he did not close the latch on top.

Everyone lined up at the door. "All right," Mrs. Hensley reminded them, "have good manners and bring me back a five."

Ms. Fudge had a discipline system. If all students in the class were good, they received a score of five. If some rules were broken the score went down. It was hard to get a five from Ms. Fudge. In fact, in the history of Ms. Fudge at

West Park, no class had ever brought back a five.

As his class filed down the hall to the gym, Kirby kept thinking of the rope. With each step the rope got longer and the ceiling higher. He shoved his hands deep down in his sweatshirt pockets and shuffled along. Kirby felt something in his pocket. Maybe it was his winter gloves. If it was his gloves, they were moving! Pulling his pocket out a bit as he walked, he peered down inside the darkness of the lining.

Oh good grief, he thought: It's Hamlet! Didn't I shut the door?

Forgetting about the rope he now worried about Hamlet. If Ms. Fudge found Hamlet, they would both be court martialed. He could imagine Ms. Fudge gleefully disposing of Hamlet. He could picture Hamlet standing with his back against the gym wall wearing a tiny white blind fold.

Down the hall he could see Ms. Fudge standing just outside the gym door. Not because she was glad to see them, but because it was the school rule. She was to see that the students didn't kill each other as they marched down the hall.

"Attention students," Ms. Fudge bellowed. "I am sorry to disappoint you today, but we will not be having the obstacle course." The

49

students clapped spontaneously.

"Quiet, class! Due to the tiles coming off the side of the gym floor, we cannot run laps. We are, therefore, forced to do the parachute."

The parachute was the kids' favorite. The process was very simple. The class arranged themselves in a big circle in the middle of the gym floor. They sat on their feet with each student holding part of the colorful striped parachute with both hands. On command, they raised their arms in unison, sending the parachute ballooning into a huge mushroom shape. On signal, every other kid let go of it and tried to run to the other side of the chute before the others pulled it down on top of them.

Seeing the parachute made Kirby feel silly for worrying all morning about PE. After all, he thought, his sweatshirt did have big pockets. Hamlet would probably sleep right through PE class.

The class had raised and lowered the chute a few times. Those holding it would laugh and those caught would scream appropriately. Kirby had made it through one time and got caught in the middle once. That time, however, he ran smack head on into Lila Smithers. It was almost worth it to see the fuss she made about her hair getting all messed up.

Kirby was holding on tight, ready to raise his arms with his class when he saw something that made his blood turn cold. Smack in the middle of the parachute was Hamlet. He took one hand and automatically felt his pocket even though he knew he would find it empty.

Before Kirby could open his mouth let alone yell something, the parachute swushed up into the air. It seemed to take hours before it floated back to the gym floor. When it did, Hamlet was gone! Kirby felt he could no longer breathe. He felt all the air in the room had been sucked out of the gym by the force of the parachute.

"Kirby Piper, what is the matter with you?" Kirby could hear the gruff voice of Ms. Fudge. "Mr. Piper, I suggest you lay back and get your breath. We are going to have to whip you into better shape if you are winded by this activity!"

Kirby lay back on the hard gym floor, inhaling much needed oxygen back into his lungs. He was staring straight up at the ceiling. That is when he spotted him.

Hamlet was sitting way up on the middle beam. He seemed completely unaware that he was more than twenty feet above the very hard gym floor. Evidently when the parachute ballooned up, Hamlet was catapulted to the beam.

"I'm fine," Kirby stammered as he scrambled up from the floor. "I'm…I'm in great shape; in fact, I'll just climb that rope and show you!"

Before Kirby could think about it and well before Ms. Fudge could react, Kirby was climbing the rope.

The rest of the students dropped the chute and gathered around the rope. When Kirby was about half way up, the kids started counting. Kirby could think only about saving his little pet. He kept his eyes fixed on Hamlet as he climbed. Hand over hand, he inched closer to the ceiling. The nearer he got to the top, the louder the class counted, "14, 15,…19…23…"

Hamlet was just sitting, as if he didn't have a care in the world. Luckily the red ribbon was hiding him from the audience below.

With his last remaining strength and courage, he grabbed Hamlet and the ribbon as the class yelled, "30!" He shoved both in his pocket and slowly slithered down the rope.

The class went wild with yelling and clapping as Kirby's feet touched the floor.

11

The Books do Battle!

Kirby got Hamlet safely back in his cage with no one the wiser. That went especially for Hamlet. Once he got a taste of true freedom, it was hard to keep him at home.

Many mornings, Kirby would come to school only to find Hamlet sitting on top of the cage instead of in it. Luckily, he was usually the first kid in the room. He tried to come early to clean Hamlet's cage. Mrs. Hensley was usually kept busy getting ready for the day.

As the days went by, Kirby stopped skipping pages when he read his books. He couldn't prove it wasn't just a coincidence, but as long as he read every word, Hamlet would peacefully rest on his shoulder. If he tried skipping, even a sentence, Hamlet headed for Kirby's tender bare neck.

Wednesday was library day. The class went just after the first bell rang. During library time, Kirby used to go straight to the shelves and try to find the skinniest book. Lately, however, he had looked for books about knights and dragons and it didn't seem important to look for the thinnest book.

Mrs. Alders was the librarian. She had reddish brown hair which she usually wore in a pony tail and brown boxy leather sandals on her feet. She had wild colorful socks to match every occasion. Her socks were always the first thing that the students looked at when they saw Mrs. Alders.

Today, she told them to hurry and take their seats because she had a special announcement for them.

"Class, I'm so excited to tell you about something called The Battle of the Books." As she went on talking, Kirby's mind wandered to the books in his desk back in his classroom.

He imagined which books he wanted to see battling each other, _Math for You_ and _Working Words_. Kirby could picture them squaring off ready for war.

The reading book was thick and heavy, but the math book taller and faster on its feet. Each rival stood cover to cover trying to stare each other down. Then each warrior drew a glimmering sword, like the knights of old used in battle.

The reading book swung first then tried to jump on the math book. The math book dodged and swung around. The reading book opened partially and hundreds of words spat out toward Math for You. As the words hit the sword, they ricocheted around the room. Each time they made contact with the cold steel, sparks flew through the air. The math book's sword came down and....

"Do you have a question?" Mrs. Alders asked, bringing Kirby back from his daydream. "You were swinging your arms in the air so much, I'm sure your question just won't wait."

"No ma'am, I guess I was just thinking of the Battle."

"Well then, I'm sure you could tell the class in your own words about Battle of the Books," said Mrs. Alders.

Kirby coughed and sputtered as he grabbed his throat, "I...I...have a frog in my throat." The class snickered.

Lila jumped up. "I'd be happy to tell everyone about the Battle of the Books, Mrs. Alders, while Kirby gets the frog out of his throat."

"All right, Lila, you do that while I pass out the book list," Mrs. Alders directed. She then began handing papers to each table.

Lila stood up and cleared her throat and began with an air of importance, "Well, it is very easy to understand if you were paying attention. Mrs. Alders is going to give us a list of ten books to read. We need to get on teams of more than one. She said more than two would be best. I think she is right, especially those of you who can't read as well as me."

Mrs. Alders gave Lila a stern teacher look. Lila continued, "Then the teachers ask us questions about the books. The teams go against teams and finally there is a champion. When it is all over, all the contestants get to have a sleepover all night in the school."

All the kids clapped and whistled at the idea of spending the night in the building. Even those who didn't particularly like it in the day time thought it would be fantastic to spend an entire night at the school.

On the way back to the classroom, Frankie walked behind Kirby.

"Hey Kirby," Frankie said in a low voice.

"Why don't we get on a team together? You don't hate books nearly as much now, do you?"

"I don't know. I never really thought about it. I sure don't love them!" Kirby responded.

"Look, I read some, you read some and we get somebody else on the team, someone real smart," Frankie said with confidence. "And besides think about the trouble we could cause if we stayed here all night!"

"Oh sure, we put out this ad that says we are looking for someone smart," said Kirby sarcastically.

Frankie rolled his eyes up at the ceiling. "All we've got to do is find someone who likes to read."

Both boys said at the same time, "Anyone but Lila Smithers!"

12

Could be a Robber!

Kirby could tell from Mrs. Hensley's face that something was wrong the minute he came into the classroom that morning.

He was putting his things away in his desk when she walked over to him.

"I thought you would be the first one in the room. I wanted to talk to you alone," she said in a solemn voice.

Kirby recognized that tone of voice; his mother used the same one when she was going to tell him something bad. Like it was time to get his shots or when she told him his sister broke his video game.

"Listen Kirby, I put off telling you this until I was really sure, but Hamlet has been getting out at night and chewing up important things in the closet," Mrs. Hensley said as she looked over at Hamlet.

"But, it can't be him. I mean, he wouldn't do that. He's a trained Hamster!" Kirby blurted out.

She led him over to the other side of the room and opened the closet door. It was full of stacked cardboard boxes. He could see that at least two boxes contained nothing but what appeared to be chewed papers. In the corner was a stack of reading books which looked like something or someone had chewed off the corners of their covers.

"But," Kirby stammered, "it might not be Hamlet. Could be a robber came in and stole some test or something and to cover it up tore up those papers!"

"I'm sorry Kirby, but I think that is very unlikely. If this happens one more time, we will have to find another home for Hamlet," said Mrs. Hensley in a kind but firm voice.

It was hard for Kirby to concentrate the rest of the day. He kept thinking about Hamlet. He had to admit the circumstantial evidence was pretty strong.

He had caught Hamlet out of his cage many times. He could believe that Hamlet might chew dumb old boxes, but nothing would convince him that Hamlet would chew up a book!

13

Finding a Teammate

Kirby tried to keep an extra eye on Hamlet, but his school day was always filled with so many things to do.

One of his first priorities was finding someone else to be on the Battle of the Books team with him and Frankie. Both boys spent the next day watching their classmates.

As it turned out, it wasn't in the classroom at all that they found their candidate. It was during last recess when Kirby had pushed Lila off the jungle gym. She wasn't hurt and according to Kirby she had stuck her tongue out at him. She ran crying and limping to the playground monitor. Lila was sent to the sick room to lie down until the end of recess.

He was walled by Mrs. Steel, the playground monitor. He had to sit against the school building. Kirby was lucky and only had the punishment of one recess. Since recess had only five minutes left when he was caught, he had a short sentence. Kirby thought it was well worth the punishment to see the look on Lila's face as she took the big dive.

Kirby leaned back against the hard wall. To his left a few feet away, he saw Harvey Betters. Harvey was reading a book.

"Hey, Harvey, what did they catch you doing?" Kirby said in a low voice.

Harvey looked up from his book momentarily to answer. "They didn't catch me doing anything. I'm here because I want to finish my book. There's never enough time to read in class."

"Yeah," said Kirby sarcastically, "I know what you mean. I just get to reading and Mrs. Hensley says times up, put your book away."

The bell rang; his sentence was over. He hurried to catch up with Frankie before he could get into the classroom.

After talking it over, both boys agreed Harvey would make a great partner.

During class, Kirby wrote a note asking Harvey to join their team. Harvey quickly agreed. He added he had already read most of the books.

This was Harvey's first year at West Park. His father worked at the Army Depot outside of town. Being in the military, his family had moved from place to place many times. Always being the new kid at school, he had not made many friends. He had spent a lot of his time alone and reading.

The three boys soon became good friends spending lots of recesses in deep discussions about the books.

Kirby and Hamlet spent most of their extra free time in class reading together.

In the evening, Kirby was reading so much that his Mom and Dad started calling him Mr. Bookworm.

He would always respond back with a grin. "Not a worm. You know I hate worms!"

That evening Uncle Louie called on the phone. He inquired about Hamlet and Kirby's reading.

Uncle Louie described how Hamlet would sit on his shoulder as he read his books in his snug log cabin. He joked that he had read Shakespeare so many times to him that he was sure Hamlet could read it himself.

14

What You Need is a Wad of Green Paper in Your Mouth!

Kirby double checked the cage every afternoon before he left the classroom for the day. Several times, however, he would come in to find the catch undone. Either he was being careless or Hamlet had found a way to open the latch.

Mrs. Hensley had a new project for the classroom. They were studying communities in Social Studies. She informed them they would be building their own city. Mrs. Hensley's husband had brought a big piece of plywood. She had drawn squares on it and called them house lots. She explained to the class that they would each be given a lot to build their own house.

They made their houses out of empty milk cartons that they saved from lunch in the cafeteria.

Kirby was glad his house was two streets over from Lila's. Even in the pretend community, he did not want to live near her. Frankie was not so lucky: his lot was right across the street from Lila.

Mrs. Hensley had what she called zoning rules. All houses were to be painted with tempera paint. Only white school glue or tape was to be used and all houses must have windows and doors. There were, however, no height restrictions. Lila Smithers was determined to have the biggest and tallest house. She had already used six milk cartons. No one could figure how she could build so high without them falling over.

Lila had tried talking Mrs. Hensley into making her the mayor of their city. Mrs. Hensley thanked her for her civic mindedness, but told her a mayor was not needed at the present time.

Kirby had two milk cartons. He had tried to make a two story house, but every morning he would come in and find the top carton had fallen off and was lying on the wooden platform. He had put so much white glue on the carton that it oozed down like some sort of eerie slime. Kirby complained that he needed better glue, but Mrs. Hensley said that he had to deal with the problem using the materials allowed by the zoning ordinance. While all this was going on, Lila Smither's house kept getting bigger and taller.

"Kirby." It was Lila. "I think you need to do something about your ratty yard. You need to put some green paper down for lawn and plant some trees or maybe flowers."

"Lila," Kirby quipped, "you need to put a big wad of green paper in your mouth and maybe some flowers!"

The following morning, Kirby came in the classroom only to find Hamlet out of his cage again. Luckily, Mrs. Hensley was in the office on an errand leaving him the only student in the room.

He had almost given up finding Hamlet before Mrs. Hensley returned when he saw Lila's high rise swaying back and forth. He rushed over and looked into the tiny curtained window. There was Hamlet curled up asleep on a couch Lila had made out of a jumbo paper clip box. He had been rolling around trying to get comfortable before he fell asleep. Kirby had to push a pencil through the window to nudge Hamlet awake. He then shoved him toward the door until Kirby could use his finger and thumb to pull him out.

"You're a naughty, naughty boy!" he scolded Hamlet.

Kirby scrambled to his feet with Hamlet clutched in his hand, just as Mrs. Hensley came through the door.

"Good morning, Kirby. I see you have your buddy there with you," greeted Mrs. Hensley in a cheery voice.

15
Closer and Closer!

The day was getting closer and closer to the Battle of the Books.

At the supper table, his mom and dad quizzed him about the books. Alexis seemed actually interested as he described the characters in the books and what was happening to them. She thought Kirby was absolutely brilliant for reading such big books.

"Miss Cook is going to teach me to read too!" she said in between bites of her spaghetti.

His mom had read a couple of the books when she was Kirby's age. She talked about them like they were her old lost friends. His parents had bought him a few of the books on the list. Kirby had scooted some of his toys off the book shelves to make room for them.

His favorite book so far was_Poppy. It was about this little mouse that battled a big scary owl. There was even a fierce sword fight in it.

Kirby and Frankie were asked to choose a name for their team. They decided to call themselves the Knight Readers. Lila's team was the Bookettes.

Lila was having big trouble with her teammates. Carlene Ditton had dropped out. She and Lila were in some sort of yelling fight every other day. Lila insisted on being the boss of the team and telling everyone what to do. Carlene had eventually told Lila to go kiss a frog.

Now Lila's team was down to her and Jeannie Whittle. Jeannie followed Lila around like a little puppy. They seemed to be the perfect pair.

In honor of the Battle of the Books, Mrs. Hensley announced a Read in Day. They were allowed to wear their pajamas and bring pillows. Kirby wore his blue and yellow Seattle Seahawks pajamas. On his feet were his well worn hound dog house shoes with floppy ears that dragged the ground.

16

Round One

Today was the long awaited first round of The Battle of the Books. Kirby had read all the books and was proud he had not skipped any pages even in those with real chapters.

The first round went very well. Frankie answered two of the questions. Kirby answered one and Harvey the rest of them. They did well enough to beat the other team. This meant they would be having at least one more round.

Lila also had a round that day. She answered every question. She never gave Jeannie a chance to open her mouth. Jeannie didn't appear to mind, but Kirby wanted to smack Lila in the chops anyway.

That afternoon, Kirby strutted home in triumph! He excitedly told his parents about the match. They told him he was king for the evening and could choose whatever he wanted for supper. That night they all had Happy Meals.

The classroom community continued to grow. Mrs. Hensley had given everyone an additional building lot. They were zoned commercial lots. This meant they had to put some sort of business on it. Kirby chose a gas station. That way he could bring some of his hot wheel cars from home. Frankie chose a bank; he said he wanted a job around money. Lila, well, she was duplicating Luxor's Boutique. She brought tiny doll clothes and accessories to stock it.

To everyone's surprise, especially Kirby, his team won every one of their rounds. The boys began strutting around like a couple of peacocks. Kirby even stopped complaining about reading.

Then just as everything in his world was looking up, kaboom, things went terribly wrong!

17

Frankly, You Don't Have the Brain Power.......

Kirby got a telephone call from Harvey. His father had just been transferred from the Army Depot to a post in Idaho. His mom was taking Harvey and leaving that weekend for their new home.

"Mom says it is real hard to get post housing and there is only one house open now. Mom and Dad are afraid if they don't take it now, someone else may get it first. If we can't live there, we have to get an apartment in town which is a lot more money," Harvey sadly explained. "I'm sorry about the Battle of the Books, but

Kirby, you and Frankie have read all the books."

Later that day, Kirby and Frankie were out at recess discussing their miseries when they saw a crowd forming by the swings. Through the crowd, they saw Mrs. Steel, the playground teacher. She was leading Lila and Jeannie to the office. It looked like Lila was going to have a black eye and Jeannie was holding a Kleenex on her own bleeding nose.

Lila was wailing how she was going to sue and Jeannie screaming Lila was a bossy cow. She added that she had taken her last orders from Lila and she could forget about her being a Bookette.

Kirby and Frankie just looked on in astonishment. They had never heard Jeannie say a complete sentence before this day. Now she was screaming like a maniac.

A little later Lila and Jeannie came back from the office. Everyone in class was dying to find out the details of what happened while they were there, but both girls just took their seats without saying a word.

After school, Lila strutted over to Kirby and Frankie.

"Hey guys, I have a proposition for you," she said in an uncharacteristic sweet voice.

"Listen, Lila, what in the world could you

have that we would want?" responded Kirby.

"Well you may not want it, but you certainly need it! You need a new person on your team. You have lost Harvey the way I hear it," said Lila with a sort of smug look on her swollen black eyed face. "We have both won exactly the same number of rounds, so Mrs. Hensley said it was okay with the rules if we combine our teams."

"We don't need anyone else!" snapped Frankie.

"Well guys, don't take this the wrong way, but you both don't have the brain power to go it alone," Lila shot back returning to her normal agitating voice.

Kirby wanted to smack her and give her matching black eyes, but he held his temper.

He said in a voice he hoped sounded confident, "Frankie and I will talk it over and get back to you."

Frankie pushed Kirby over to the other side of the walk way. "Kirby, we just can't be on the same team with that lizard Lila."

"I know I feel the same way too, but let's think this thing through. We both have put a lot of work and sweat to get this far," Kirby said thoughtfully.

After several minutes of arguing and a lot

of hard thinking, both boys agreed as distasteful as it was, they needed Lila. They flipped a coin. Frankie lost the toss. He had to tell Lila she could be on the team.

18
And the Winner is…….

At last, the final round of the Battle of the Books to determine the champions. The school was buzzing with excitement. It was going to take place in the gym. All the classes were allowed to watch the matches. PE was even canceled so they could use the gym. It was the only room at West Park big enough for the student body and it had the added advantage of a stage. Close to the front of the stage the teachers had placed two long folding tables. A pitcher of ice water with glasses had been placed on each table where the contestants were to sit. A big banner was hung on the wall behind them. In big gold letters it read,

Battle of the Books

An old wooden podium was separating the two tables.

Kirby and Frankie dressed for a regular day of school. He had remembered to wear his lucky soccer shirt. Lila on the other hand looked like a nine year old lawyer. She was wearing a dark blue wool skirt, white blouse and white striped pullover sweater. She had black shoes with shiny gold buckles. Her heels were higher than she normally wore, which caused her to sway unsteadily on her feet.

She had a matching black leather purse hanging over her shoulder. Kirby couldn't be sure but he thought she was even wearing some makeup. Her cheeks looked a funny reddish color and her eye lashes were extra black and fluffy. Her long blond hair, as usual, hung straight down her back.

Frankie jabbed Kirby in the ribs and whispered, "There is no way I am sitting next to Lila!"

"Hold your horses right there. If you think I'm going to have her beside me you are just plain nuts!" shot back Kirby.

"There is only one solution and that is she sits next to both of us. We put her in the middle.!"

"How is it going to be better for us both to suffer?" Frankie wailed.

"Look, we are both in this together. Besides, if we look straight ahead neither one of us will have to look at her. We'll pretend she is Harvey." Kirby tried to say it with a straight face.

"Oh yeah, like that's going to happen!" Frankie said moaning.

Kirby took his place at the table. He looked out into the audience. The younger grades were on the floor on mats in front and older students behind them on chairs. He could see Alexis down below on the floor sitting with her class.

The teachers were trying to get students seated in a quiet and orderly fashion. So far, they weren't totally successful. They had stationed themselves among the students for crowd control.

After a few minutes, Mr. Bunders, the principal, came up to the podium. He was carrying a gray metal box. He sat it down in front of him.

"Students, welcome to our annual Battle of the Books. In a few moments, we will begin. The audience needs to be very quiet while the questions are being asked and answered. Mrs. Alders, our very own librarian, will ask the questions."

As Mrs. Alders was walking up the steps

to the stage, Alexis called out, "Hey Kirby I'm down here! She was waving both hands. Then she proudly announced to her class, "That's my brother Kirby!"

Kirby could feel his face turning bright red. The audience snickered.

"Good morning, everyone. I want to welcome all of you to our annual Battle of the Books. I will ask twenty questions, drawing them at random from this box. Once the battle begins, we will continue until we have a winner. If a team member must leave for any reason, their team-mates will carry on without him. Today, we will have the final match between the Green Hornets and the Knight Readers. Good luck to both teams."

With that, Mrs. Alders broke the seal on the question box and reached into the container.

Kirby glanced over at the Green Hornets. They had two boys and two girls on their team. He wondered if they had butterflies in their stomachs like he did. Kirby's throat felt like he had swallowed Spongebob. He needed a drink. He leaned over to pour a glass of water and his hand slipped, spilling water all over Lila. You would have thought it was hot soup the way she reacted.

She jumped up shrieking, "You clumsy

oaf! You stupid, stupid! This outfit has to be dry cleaned! If I get a stain on it you'll be sorry!"

She stomped out trying to look dignified, but with her unsteady feet and dripping with water she was not very successful. Kirby assumed Lila was headed for the bathroom to dry off. *That Lila is such a cry baby,* he thought.

The teams had tossed a coin before the match and the Green Hornets were to get the first question. Kirby was getting very nervous. What if Lila doesn't get back in time?

He was glad his team did not have to go first. At least this would give them some additional time for Lila to get back. He kept looking at the door for her.

The Green Hornets answered correctly. Mrs. Alders reached into the box for another question and turned to the Knight Readers. "What was the name of Amy's sister in The Dollhouse Murders?"

Frankie blurted out, "I know it, and her name was Louann!"

"Correct," Mrs. Alders said with a smile.

The battle continued. Question by question each team battled for the title. Frankie gave a majority of the answers for the team. Kirby had been content to answer two of them. He thought he could hear his heart skip a beat when he gave an answer.

He kept hoping he would see Lila come through the door. *I can't believe I would ever be wishing for Lila to be in the same room, let alone beside me,* thought Kirby.

He was brought back from his thoughts by the voice of Mrs. Alders. "For the championship of the Battle of the Books the question is…what is the Latin name of the porcupine in the book <u>Poppy</u>?"

The gym was totally silent. Kirby could hear his heart beating against his soccer shirt.

Frankie looked over at Kirby. He could tell by the blank expression on Frankie's face he did not know the answer.

Kirby took a deep breath and then with a shaky voice said, "His name was Erethizon Dordatum."

Kirby sat without breathing. *Where did that answer come from?* he wondered. *It just jumped out of my mouth! Why didn't I keep my mouth shut?*

He had never known the gym to be so quiet. It seemed like hours before Mrs. Alders finally turned to the audience.

"I present to you the new Battle of the Books winners, the Knight Readers!" Her voice was almost drowned out by applause from the audience.

Mrs. Alders placed a red, white and blue ribbon with a golden medallion around the boy's neck. Then she gave each boy a big hug.
The boys gave each other high fives as the audience applauded loudly. They ran around the table and shook hands with the members of the Green Hornets. They were receiving silver medallions for second place.

In the meantime…

Lila had been fuming mad by the time she got to the bathroom. A puddle of water was starting to form under her black leather shoes with the gold buckles. She would have to take her sweater off. *After all,* she thought, *I do have my designer Maggie Jones blouse underneath my sweater.*

Forgetting to take her shoulder purse off, she tried pulling her sweater over her head. Her purse got tangled around her neck. The clasp snapped open and a tiny plastic bottle fell out. The bottle cap flipped off in all the pulling and twisting. The contents of the bottle leaked onto Lila's sweater.

Lila tried pulling the sweater up over her shoulders. The clothes, however, would not budge off of her head. Her hair, purse and sweater were all stuck in one big jumbled wad around her head. Lila yanked and tugged. The more she struggled, the more it became a tangled mess.

She could not see with her sweater covering her eyes. She gave one gigantic and frantic tug and her hands slipped. She was flung back against the door of the bathroom stall. As the swinging door gave way to her weight, she was hurled backward. She lost her footing and her rear end landed in the toilet. Now it wasn't just her sweater that was all wet!

Kirby and Frankie stayed in the gym while all the classes went back to their rooms. Mr. Bunders wanted to get some pictures of Mrs. Alders giving awards to both teams.

It was recess by the time they were walking back to their classrooms. A familiar voice stopped them in the hall.

"Hey Kirby." It was Jeannie. "Did you hear what happened to Lila? Seems Mr. Fender went to clean the bathroom and found Lila in there kicking and screaming on the floor. Evidently she had super glue in her purse and it got stuck in her hair. She must have been using it on her milk carton in our class community project."

"That must be how she could get her house so tall," Frankie added.

"And mine kept falling apart using white school glue!" Kirby said sounding annoyed.

"So what's going to happen to Lila?" both boys said at once.
"Well, all I know is her mom came and got her out of the bathroom. I overheard her mom say she was taking her to the beauty shop to get her sweater cut out of her hair," Jeannie pretended to shutter.

19

What's this....She Gasped!

Kirby could hardly wait for the sleepover. Tonight it was actually happening. He was so excited he could barely eat his supper. His mom was hoping to get some wholesome food in him before he left for school. She knew once he got there he would be snacking on junk until he fell asleep.

Kirby, on the other hand, was sure he would be awake all night. As far as good food went, Kirby had his backpack filled with nutritious food such as Rice Krispy Treats, m&m's, popcorn balls, chocolate chip cookies and Kool Aid Jammers. He thought it felt strange to be so excited about going to school.

His mom dropped him off at the school with his sleeping bag and backpack filled with all his goodies. His parents had even let him bring the digital camera to take pictures of the evening. Although he was right on time, there were already several kids who evidently arrived early.

Kirby had spent many a day in this building but it looked and felt completely different in the evening.

He could hear balls bouncing on the floor of the gym. He thought he'd try that place out first. When he entered, he could see kids running around shooting baskets and playing tag. Mr. Bunders was at one end of the gym struggling to put down some blue mats for the kids to sit and play board games.

"Hey Kirby!" He recognized that voice. It was Frankie calling from across the gym. Frankie had a basketball in his hand and was poised ready to try for a basket. "Isn't it cool, we can have recess all night?"

Kirby felt better seeing Frankie. The ball missed the basket and Frankie let it roll across the floor. He ran over to Kirby. "Let's go check this place out. We need to get the lay of the land so we know all the happening places around here."

"Okay," said Kirby as he gave Frankie a high five, "but you know we have all night."

It was darker now, which made the building look bigger and somewhat eerie. In spite of all the kids, the halls still echoed like they were empty. Kirby saw shadows on the walls he had never noticed in the daytime. His footsteps sounded loudly on the tiled floor.

Kirby and Frankie saw Lila. She was playing a Barbie board game with two other girls. Lila was whining that she should get an extra roll of the dice because it had hit one girl's foot.

"Listen Frankie, there is something we ought to do." He steered Frankie over to the wall and whispered something to him."

The look on Frankie's face showed astonishment, then finally a nodding of his head yes.

"Okay," said Frankie, "we better hurry and do this or I'm going to chicken out!"

They sauntered over to Lila. The Barbie board game had evidently broken up by then. She was just coming out of the girls' bathroom. Kirby had the feeling she was in there primping and foo fooing her hair.

"Hey Lila, we got something for you," Kirby muttered. He hated the thought of anyone thinking he was giving something to Lila.

Kirby gritted his teeth. He was determined to do this no matter how obnoxious Lila acted. His feet wanted to turn around in the other direction. Without saying a word, Kirby shoved a small box into Lila's hand.

"What's this?" Lila sputtered.

Lila hesitated as she slowly opened the box. She was trying to prepare herself in the event something jumped out. She didn't trust that Kirby and Frankie. *What are those jokers up to?* she wondered.

When Lila slid the top off the box, she was staring at a golden medallion.

"W…what's this?" she gasped.

"It's the medallion that we won for Battle of the Books," said Kirby.

"What do you mean, I didn't win anything. I was…was…indisposed," Lila stammered.

"Lila, you were still on our team. Just because you were…were…indisposed doesn't mean you weren't on the team. We asked Mrs. Alders to give us a medallion for you."

Lila clutched the medallion to her chest. "It does look good with my eyes, don't you think?" She was actually smiling at the boys.

"Whatever," Kirby muttered. This situation was getting entirely too mushy for his liking.

"Well, we'll see you around Lila, come on Frankie we got stuff to do and people to see."

Frankie and Kirby scooted down the hall without looking back.

20

Teeth that looked like Long Cold Icicles!

Hamlet was fast asleep in room 18. He had found a real cushy spot in Lila's milk carton house. She had recently put some cotton in the staple box and then covered it in bright green velvet material. Once Hamlet had found this spot, he considered it his space.

Every evening, after the custodian had finished cleaning the room, Hamlet would use his little paws to undo the catch on his cage. Then standing on the Ferris wheel, he was able to crawl to freedom. From there, it was easy to make his way across the shelf. He would descend the bookcase by using Mrs. Hensley's convenient sweater hanging on a hook. From there, it was only one tiny hop to land on the community platform.

Tonight, Hamlet was dreaming of scampering in a valley of carrots when he awoke to scratching sounds. His eyes snapped open just as he heard a loud crash. Peering out of the window of Lila's house, he could make out some sort of animal on Mrs. Hensley's desk.

Suddenly, "kerplop," the top of Kirby's milk carton fell off and tumbled loudly to the wooden platform. Evidently the glue wasn't completely dry from the last time Kirby had slapped it on his house.

The scrunchy sound stopped and the animal looked up, sniffing the air. Trembling, Hamlet forced himself to peek out of the window. He was looking at a monstrous rat! The animal was a least six inches long. Adding his tail to his length would stretch him to be at least a foot.

The swift rat immediately leaped through the air and landed on a student desk close to Hamlet. Without hesitation, the savage rodent jumped to the ground and bounded across the room to the milk carton community.

His heart racing, Hamlet scampered out of the high-rise and headed down the main street. The villainous rodent was now within inches of catching him. Hamlet's only advantage at the moment was his size. He could scamper inside some of the houses to escape the rat, giving him a few precious seconds to catch his breath.

The brutal rat reached in through the windows with his clawed paws. Waving them about wildly, he tried to get his clutches on Hamlet.

At one point, Hamlet ran into Lila's Boutique, sending racks of clothes flying.

He squeezed out the back door and scurried down the street. He hopped off the platform and onto a bookcase.

The rat was in hot pursuit. Hamlet sped past a long line of social studies books. As the rat sprinted across the bookcase, he pulled a gray metal bookend over causing the books to fall toward him like dominoes.

To save himself, the rat spring to the ground. This gave Hamlet a chance to climb up onto the paper cutter. The persistent rat raced around to the other side of the book shelves, hoping to trap Hamlet.

Hamlet could see the rat's top lip, which was curled back showing his sharp ugly teeth. By the light of the street lamp coming though the window, his teeth looked like long cold icicles.

The nimble rat jumped on the paper cutter with Hamlet. He snarled wickedly at Hamlet, thinking at last he had caught his prey! The additional weight, however, sent the paper cutter crashing to the floor.

As the cutter tumbled down, its cutting arm flew up. The sharp cutting blade sliced behind Hamlet. It brushed against his skin. Hamlet was so startled, he froze for a second. He was trying to remember if he had a tail or not. He only hoped he didn't because he didn't have one now!

The rat was a little stunned itself. He lay on his back for a second before he jumped up and shook his head. He snarled at Hamlet. Hamlet shivered back at him.

In desperation, Hamlet darted to the curtain and began climbing up toward the ceiling. He wasn't sure where he was going, but he figured it was to his advantage to get farther from the floor.

The hideous ugly rat moved with lightning speed. He bounded on top of Mrs. Hensley's desk. The chewed papers from her book went flying into the air. The fearless rat made a mighty leap to the curtain, but not judging the distance correctly, he tumbled to the floor.

The rat grabbed the bottom of the curtain with his teeth. He began shaking his head and snarling vigorously as if he was trying to kill it. Trembling, Hamlet dug his little paws into the material, but it was getting harder and harder for him to hang onto the curtain. The rat gave one tremendous tug and Hamlet was sent spiraling to the floor. Luckily, he was not hurt as he landed on the overhead projector.

Hamlet was flailing his arms and legs wildly. His back foot accidentally caught the switch of the projector. The machine clicked on, almost blinding Hamlet by its glaring white light. The lamp from the projector heated the smooth glass under his feet. In any other circumstance, he might have found this warm spot a perfect place to curl up for a nap.

Across the room, the tireless rat was startled by a gigantic hamster walking on the back cabinet. The hamster appeared to be at least five feet tall. He had a huge furry head and fat balloon shaped body. Hamlet's tiny paws were now as big as the rat's entire body.

The rat was terrified for the first time in its life. Hamlet's silhouette was being projected on the wall, transforming him into a fierce giant hamster.

21

Back in the Gym

Back in the gym, Kirby and Frankie had just finished three bags of m&m's and a Kool Aide Jammer. They were irritating people by taking candid pictures of almost everyone. Kirby snapped a good one of Lila sleeping with her mouth open and her short hair sticking straight out from her head like a blond porcupine.

"I bet Lila would give us a million bucks for that picture," Frankie chuckled.

"Hey, Frankie, I got an idea! Let's go see Hamlet," said Kirby.

"That's a great idea! Let's go find the custodian and see if he will let us in the room," Frankie said with renewed excitement.

Both boys knew Mr. Fender would let

them in the classroom. He was always feeding the school animals. One time, he told Kirby that Hamlet really liked his wife's recipe for turnips. A few minutes later all three headed down to room 18.

As the custodian opened the classroom door, the first thing Kirby saw was Hamlet sparing like a prize fighter on top of the overhead projector. He jabbed with his left paw, then his right. His foot work matched his jabs. Hamlet was gaining confidence with each punch.

A noise startled the boys, causing them to turn around. They saw the once fierce rat cowering in the corner of the room. The rat had not taken his eyes off of the gigantic image of Hamlet on the wall and was not aware that anyone else had entered the room.

"Well, howdy, if this isn't some sight to behold!" Mr. Fender said as he slowly and cautiously crept toward a metal waste can. With the boys watching, neither being able to speak or move, Mr. Fenders slammed the trash can over the frightened rat.

"Gottcha!" he exclaimed as the can touched down around the startled rat.

At the sound of the can, the boys ran to Hamlet. Kirby scooped up the hamster and Frankie ran to switch on the classroom lights.

"From the looks of this room these guys must have been having some party! I got a feeling this critter has been the one chewing up things in your teacher's closet," Mr. Fender pointed out as he quickly turned the trash can right side up, trapping the rat deep down in the bottom.

Both boys ran over to look down inside the can. "He sure looks vicious huh, Mr. Fender," said Kirby.

"Well," answered the custodian, "he probably is thinking the same thing about you kids right about now."

"What's going to happen to him?" questioned Kirby.

"I'll come back later and get him. I'll take him by that big grove of willow trees near Miller's Lake. He can make his home there where there are no closets full of papers and for his sake no overhead projectors."

Kirby placed Hamlet gently in his cage. He rubbed his furry little head as he told him to sleep tight. Then, as an after thought, he placed a heavy reading book on top the cage to insure the trap door stayed closed, at least for one night. Kirby yawned and Frankie rubbed his eyes.

They trudged happily back to the main building with Mr. Fender.

22

We have a Problem!

The following Monday as Kirby entered the classroom, the first thing that met his eyes was a gigantic purple and gold banner hanging across the blackboard. In big red letters was written,

Our Hero Hamlet!

Mrs. Hensley was standing by Hamlet's cage, "I understand Hamlet was innocent and officially cleared of all chewing charges. Mr. Fender told me all about the terrible rat and how our brave Hamlet protected our classroom. He is now the official guard hamster of room 18. This classroom is now his home as long as he wants to live here. We do have one slight problem, however," Mrs. Hensley said dramatically.

"What's that?" said Kirby afraid to hear

the answer.

"Well," she went on, "I'm afraid that nasty old rat ate all of this afternoon's lesson plans." She paused for a few seconds. "I guess we will just have to spend this afternoon having a popcorn party in honor of Hamlet's heroism!"

That is exactly what happened. They pigged out on popcorn, played board games, and listened to Mrs. Hensley read stories. Hamlet, when he wasn't sleeping on his bright green velvet couch, made of a staple box, was also munching on popcorn. Seems Lila had been very agreeable to giving the couch to Hamlet after Kirby promised to delete her not so perfect picture from the camera.

Thoughts of the Piper's Curse ran through Kirby's mind. *I think I may have beaten that old curse with the help of my buddy over there.* He looked over at Hamlet's cage. He winked at Hamlet and this time he knew that Hamlet winked back.

The End

QUICK ORDER FORM

Telephone Orders: Call 541-567-0886

E-Mail Order: hashcraftz1@charter.net

Fax Orders: 541-567-0569

Postal Order: Wordseed Publishing
Carolyn Ashcraft
650 NE 2nd Street
Hermiston, Oregon 97838

Hamlet Goes to School....... US $5.99
Plus Shipping $2.00